# ONLY *One* NIGHT

*A.R. Rose*

## A.R. ROSE

# OTHER TITLES BY A.R. ROSE

## Ridgewood Series
Between the Flames
Wicked Games We Play
Marked By Cain

## Standalones
Wreck Me
Only One Night

## Twisted Heroes
Siren

*To all the good girls who want to be bad, if only for one night.*

Only One Night is a contemporary romance novelette created for adults. This story depicts dark adult scenes and situations.

Reader discretion is advised. Only One Night contains content that may be triggering for some.

Your mental health matters. For a full list of content warnings please visit www.authorarrose.com/content-warnings.

For those of you ready to begin, I hope you enjoy ❤

H ello, Little Devil.
    The story you're about to read was created for you, the reader, to be able to live out your Halloween fantasies through the pages of this book. The female main character remains nameless and description-less, with minimal details of her life mentioned, so you can envision her any way you choose.

    Make yourself the main character. Live out your mask kinks and your stranger kinks. Even your low-key dub-con kinks lie within these pages.

    The male main character in this book has also been left nameless, so you can call him whatever your heart desires.

    But be warned, the story you are about to read is not a romance—you will not get your happily ever after. You will be left hot and bothered, and likely confused and pissed off. Set aside everything you think you know about my work, and have an open mind.

    Now, go on and be a good little slut, and enjoy the ride.
    XO,
    A.R. Rose

# CHAPTER ONE

S tarting over when you've only been with one man your entire adult life is intimidating.

My ex-husband and I were together for over fourteen years when he went and stuck his dick in his co-worker, throwing away everything we'd built.

Ten minutes was all it took for everything to shatter.

And that's all he could last, anyway—ten minutes. If he even made it that long.

He was a selfish lover, but I hadn't realized it until we divorced and I started to go out on dates. The first time I gave myself to another man was the first time I realized what I'd been missing.

Now that we're divorced, *I'm* the selfish lover. Either you make me come on your tongue or on your fingers, but until I do, your dick isn't allowed inside of me.

Period.

The best part? Not a single man I've been with has argued.

Not that I've been with many, but over the last seven months of being a single woman I've slept with three men. Four total, which in my lifetime is a very small number, but better than just the one.

I've really spread my wings since leaving my cheating piece of shit husband.

In some capacity.

Some old habits die hard, though. Like the fact that I'm a complete homebody and prefer the company of my TV or a good book, and a glass of wine, over going out with friends.

Or the fact that I'm at home alone on a Saturday afternoon, sweating my ass off in the garden.

Not that I actually *know* how to garden, but I'm absolutely going to try. Even if I end up with a bunch of dead plants and a couple hundred dollars down the drain.

When I first found this house listed for rent, I was hesitant to sign the lease. Although I loved the modest two bedroom, two bathroom house, I wasn't sure living in the middle of suburbia was the right choice for a newly single woman. But once I toured it and caught sight of the backyard, I couldn't sign fast enough.

Even now, six months later, the backyard is still my favorite thing about the house. It has a beautiful swimming pool and built-in jacuzzi, three rows of raised garden beds, and two large trees that were already prepped for a hammock.

The back fence is metal with open rungs, allowing for a full view of the mountain backdrop. It's picturesque. Sunsets here are amazing, and I spend far too many nights with a book, watching the sun go down.

The neighborhood is quiet, which is something I'm grateful for. I work long days immersed in constant chatter. The simplicity of coming home to a quiet house in a quiet neighborhood is another reason I choose to live in suburbia. My neighbors on either side are both older, and while friendly, they keep to themselves.

I prefer it that way.

Especially on days like today. Everything but the light breeze is quiet as I work beneath the fall sun, planting small, leafy vegetable plants in my garden beds. It's a little late in the season to transplant, and in reality, I'll probably forget to water them and they'll die before they've really had the chance to thrive. But still, the act of gardening brings me joy.

With soil covering my hands, I reach up and wipe a bead of sweat from my forehead using my arm. It's unseasonably warm this Halloween, and the cool, shimmering water from the pool calls to me.

I'll never get over the simple luxury of having a pool in my backyard.

Glancing over at the remaining plants still sitting in their plastic sleeves from the nursery, I decide to take a little break and walk over to the hose on the side of the house. Turning it on, I rinse the dirt off my hands.

Once finished, I go to the pool's edge and dip my foot

in the water, testing its temperature. I haven't turned the heater on, not wanting to pay the high electricity bill that comes with using it, and I know the water is going to be frigid deeper down.

Still, I peel my loose fitting, slouchy top and yoga pants off my body, dropping them into a heap by my lounge chair. My white bra and boy shorts will end up sticking to me like a second skin, but with no one around, I find it hard to care.

Without another thought, I inhale a deep breath and hold it, then dive into the deep end.

Immediately, the ice-cold water envelops me, numbing my skin as I swim deeper. Within seconds, I reach the bottom and touch the gritty PebbleTec, running my fingers across it before righting myself and pushing off with my feet.

When I breach the surface, I take in the air and push my hair back, keeping my legs moving so I stay afloat. The sun beats down against my now cold skin as I float in the water, turning on to my back. My eyes close and behind them, light from the sun dances across the darkness. The only sound is from the water sloshing gently from my hands, gliding through it.

I love this. The solidarity. The quiet.

When I was married, there was always noise. My ex hated a quiet house, so the TV or radio were always on. Not even at night did I get my silence. He slept with a fan going, and a sound machine of rainforest sounds, claiming he couldn't relax if there wasn't some sort of noise.

Nevermind what *I* needed in order to relax.

I feel myself drifting closer to the pool's edge, so I let my body disengage from the floating position and into a stand. Pulling myself out of the water, I sit on the edge, leaving my legs dangling in while I lay back on my elbows.

Sneaking a glance down, I see my white cotton bra and panty set leave absolutely nothing to the imagination. Goosebumps cover my flesh, and my nipples harden beneath the soaking wet scraps of fabric covering me. My only reprieve is the sun's kiss as it beats down on me, seeming to work extra hard to warm me up.

I relax here for a good five minutes with my eyes closed before a prickling of awareness jolts through me, and I feel like I'm being watched. It's a feeling I've never had while in the comfort of my own backyard, and it's a bit jarring.

Hesitantly, I sit up, opening my eyes as I look around. All seems calm—not a single movement or breeze sounds through the mountainside, and my backyard is empty.

But as I lay back on my elbows again and my head tilts up, I startle.

There's a man standing on my neighbor's roof, and he's staring at me.

# CHAPTER TWO

A gasp catches in my throat, and as it does, the man lifts his sunglasses to rest on top of his head. He's too far for me to catch the color of his eyes, but from what I can see from this distance, he's gorgeous.

His skin is deeply tanned, as though he's been working under the sun for months, and his arms are covered in tattoos. His hair is cropped short, and it's hard to tell from here if he has a short beard or just a five o'clock shadow, but regardless, it's working for him. He's muscular from manual labor, his shirtless chest rippling with cut ridges on display for my own private show.

I want to lick him.

There's something in the way he's looking at me that sets my body alight and all I can think about is the way this man would feel against my skin.

I wonder how big his dick is.

Does he know how to use it?

Of course he does. He literally looks like sex, and passion, and pleasure wrapped up in one.

And the way he's looking at me makes me think he may be thinking about me in a similar way.

Feeling bold, I pull my hair from behind my neck and squeeze the water out of it, letting the droplets drip between my breasts.

I know what he sees. Through my transparent clothes, he can see everything, and for some reason, I'm okay with that.

Maybe it's because I know he's over there, on my neighbor's roof, and I'm here. Or maybe it's because I'm horny as hell.

Either way, I feel like I'm having an out-of-body experience as I spread my legs apart, brace my feet against the pool's edge, and lay back.

I'm not sure why I do it, but it makes me feel liberated, when in reality, I should not be flashing this man a full view of my pussy, even if it is semi-covered by my pool-soaked panties.

Bringing my hands up to cup my breasts, I close my eyes, envisioning that man here beside me, running his hands along my body.

I don't touch myself. I *won't* touch myself.

But the weight of his gaze is enough to make me want to.

Peeking beneath my lashes, I look through my bent knees and see that the man is now squatting down on the roof, staring at me with open desire.

It makes me feel sexy.

My clit is throbbing, begging for me to slip my fingers down and relieve the edge. I'm tempted, *so* tempted, and as if he knows, I see his tongue dart out and wet his lips.

As if they have a mind of their own, my hand flutters down and my fingers brush against the fabric against my clit, pushing a moan past my lips.

My mind rages a war against itself, desperate to let all my inhibitions go and just push my fingers in my panties and do what I'm longing to do, but I also know it's wrong... so wrong.

And not me. *At all.*

*Maybe that's why it's so enticing.*

Moving my hand to the top of the cotton, I barely push my fingertips past the elastic when I hear a voice shout, and another man appears, climbing over the other side of the roof. The man who was watching me stands at the sound of the other guy's voice, giving him his attention.

The interruption sparks urgency inside me, and I sit up and fling myself back into the pool so the new man doesn't see me.

With a *splash* I break the surface and am underwater, swimming down deep. Once again, the frigid temperature curls around my body, settling its iciness in my bones.

I stay underwater until my lungs are burning and only then do I swim to the surface, draw in a hasty breath once my face hits air, then push back down. My legs kick behind me as I make my way to the shallow end and sit on the bottom of the pool, my head and shoulders settling out of the water as I catch my breath.

Pushing some droplets away from my eyes, I glance back at my neighbor's house, expecting to find the man still looking at me, but this time, he's gone.

# CHAPTER THREE

H
e stays on my mind throughout the night, haunting my memory while I sit in my house, going through the motions as though this afternoon never happened.

It *feels* like it didn't.

And if it wasn't for the fact that I am still horny as hell, I'd think I made the entire thing up.

Stirring my pasta mindlessly, I keep the water moving so it doesn't boil over. Homemade Alfredo simmers on the small burner in the back, while a single chicken breast sits on the grill pan that's cooling on my left. Exhaustion overtook me earlier, so I chose to make my life easy and defrost a few pieces of broccoli by tossing them into the sauce earlier, not wanting to dirty another pan.

After sprinkling a little more salt and pepper into the sauce, I turn off all the burners and begin to assemble my dinner into a deep, oversized bowl. Alfredo with broccoli and chicken is my favorite meal—my *comfort* meal—and I have a bottle of Moscato in the refrigerator ready to accompany it.

When everything is finally ready for consumption, I cozy myself onto my gray sectional and grab my favorite blanket, draping it over me before balancing the bowl on my lap.

As I settle in, I look around the living room and admire the cozy Halloween decor. Pumpkin scented candles flicker. Chic velvet pumpkins line my entertainment center. A black lace runner with a vintage ceramic haunted house centerpiece sits on my coffee table.

Understated.

Simple, but perfect.

After my afternoon swim, I rinsed off and dressed in yoga pants and my favorite Halloween T-shirt for the holiday. It's as good as it's going to get—it's been years since I've worn an actual costume.

Sipping my wine, I turn the TV on and pull up one of my many streaming services to find a movie that's suspenseful, so it still gives me bragging rights that I watched a scary movie on Halloween.

My porch light is off, but a small bowl of candy sits on the floor in the alcove outside, just in case a child wanders up to trick-or-treat. Doubtful, since a few neighbors warned me that we don't get many down our street, but I didn't want to be *that* house, either.

The opaque, white curtains around my living room are drawn, enclosing me in my space and setting me up for my movie night. It's pitch black outside, no moon, but the idea of someone standing outside my window scares the hell out of me. I've seen enough horror flicks, and I was taking zero chances, though the sheerness of the curtains contradicts that statement.

But I love them, so they stay.

Taking a bite of my Alfredo, I turn on *Signs*, which isn't exactly a scary movie but spooky enough that it sets the tone.

My food disappears quickly and by the time I'm finished, it feels like my stomach is about to explode.

Yawning, I sink into the couch further and relax, my eyes heavy.

I force myself to watch the movie attentively, though my eyes bounce open and closed as I attempt to stay awake and focus on the story. I know the plot well, having watched this movie several times, but it never fails to creep me out. After it first released, my best friend and I rewatched it and drank so much we ended up making tin-foil hats halfway through to wear.

We looked ridiculous and loved every second of it.

I'm nodding off, fighting against the urge to fall asleep. The movie is just nearing the first jump scare, so I straighten up on the couch, ready for it, and keep my eyes trained to the screen despite the way they ache to close.

My food is long gone, the bowl still resting on my lap, and I grip it in my hands as my heart accelerates slightly.

I should turn a light on—it'll help keep my closing eyes open and make me feel less anxious over the movie—but that would require getting up.

It's about to happen—the jump scare—and my heart rate accelerates as I wait.

Unexpectedly, the doorbell rings, and I jump, sitting ramrod straight. From my sudden movements, my bowl and spoon clatter to the floor.

*Thank goodness for the carpet.*

My heart thunders in my chest, racing beneath my rib cage as I sit frozen on my couch. Swallowing thickly, I stand, and the blanket falls from my lap and pools at my feet.

The doorbell rings again.

My body catches up before my mind does and I make my way to the door. Pulling aside the curtain of the thin window that spans the length of the front door aside, I peer through and am met with darkness.

Not a shred of light illuminates the porch, and I see nothing.

No one.

Not a shadow.

No movement.

I blow out a shaky breath and let the curtain fall from my hand, but make no move to walk away. Instead, I stand there and wait to see if the doorbell rings again. My heart beats wildly, but begins to slow with each passing moment.

Pulling myself out of the trance, I go back to the couch and pick up the remote. The idea of returning to my scary movie sounds awful, so instead, I turn the TV off and head to my en suite in my bedroom.

The house is quiet as I stand in front of my bathtub,

contemplating taking a bath. It's why I walked in here, but I took a shower this afternoon after my impromptu dip in the pool.

My thoughts return to the man on the roof. The way his skin glistened from a layer of sweat. How his eyes dragged along my body. The way he lowered himself to a squat to watch me intensely.

I know I'll never see him again, but the memory of him instantly turns me on.

Deciding to forgo the bath, I crawl into bed and open the drawer of my bedside table, looking in at my various options for boyfriends tonight.

The Rose. The Womanizer. The Wand.

I end up reaching for my Rabbit.

Settling back against my pillows, I push my lace cheeky panties down and kick out of them and my pants, before bringing my feet flat on the bed. My knees drop and I bring my toy beneath the blanket.

If there's any way to ease my nerves, this will do it.

With the click of a button, my Rabbit comes to life and I insert it, sliding it into my pussy until the smaller arm of the toy rests against my clit.

Immediately, I'm writhing against my bed, moving the toy slightly to create the friction and movement my body so desperately craves.

But it's not enough.

Several pleasurable minutes pass and I'm no closer to orgasm than I was before I turned on the toy. The pleasure is stagnant. Enough to make my body hum, but not enough to push me toward release.

Increasing the vibration, I move the toy inside of me faster and rougher, and picture the man from the roof.

It's *his* cock thrusting inside me.

*His* fingers against my clit.

Squeezing my eyes shut, I envision him vividly, but the more I let my mind act out the fantasy of him between my legs, the *less* pleasure I feel.

Frustrated, I pull the toy away from me and out from beneath the blankets, flinging it across the room.

"Ughhhh!" I groan. Reaching back under the blanket that suddenly feels stifling, I yank my clothing back up my legs, flip over onto my side, and shut my eyes.

When my breathing evens out, I relax further into my pillow and will my mind to turn off.

My day plays out in my mind like a movie, recounting everything that happened between first jumping into the pool and the doorbell ringing. A nagging feeling settles deep in my gut, telling me something is off.

But, what?

That there was a man on my neighbor's roof who made me feel desired and sexy even though he literally did nothing but *watch* me?

Or the fact that I have no idea who he is, what his name is, his relationship status...I know literally nothing about him, yet I *crave* him.

I crave the thought of him. The idea of him.

He gives my body chills. The most delicious, sensual, pulse-racing chills.

And then there was tonight...

My doorbell rang, but no one was there.

Was it him?

The logical explanation is that it was trick-or-treaters. It's Halloween, and it's late. Teenagers play pranks.

I'm pretty sure I doorbell ditched a time or two as a high schooler.

*That* made the most sense.

Yet, there is still a small part of me that wants it to be *him*. I want him to come to me.

I visualize myself opening the door and he collides his lips to mine as he pushes me backward so he can come inside, slamming the door behind him.

I picture his hands wrapping along the hem of my shirt and dragging it up, breaking our kiss just long enough so he can pull it over my head. He tosses it to the floor before returning his fingers to my shorts and pushes them, along with my panties, down my legs.

Then I'd be bare in front of him. Naked, with my nipples peaked and my pussy dripping.

He'll tug me to the kitchen and prop me on the counter before spreading my legs wide, pulling my ass to the very edge. Tilting me backward, he'll lay me down, the granite cool against my back.

And as he dips his head down, he'll stare at me while the first swipe of his tongue sweeps through the mess his stare is creating between my legs.

Licking me relentlessly, he'll swirl his tongue around my clit and drive his finger into me, enjoying the noises the wetness of my juices creates. Over and over, adding a second finger, then a third, until I come so hard I scream out into the darkness of my home.

Then I picture him carrying me to my bed, the same bed in which I lie now, my eyes heavy, and my pussy throbbing for a relief only he can grant.

# CHAPTER FOUR

Startled out of sleep, my eyes fly open when a cold hand clamps over my mouth and a firmness presses against my hips. A man is straddling me, his face cloaked in shadow from the darkness and the hood of his sweatshirt. His fingernails dig into my cheek with care—not hard enough to hurt, but enough to give a warning.

Instinct tells me to scream and as I thrash against his hand, I do, but it's muffled, and I know it makes no difference since I live alone.

I stop moving, letting my eyes adjust, and search for the face beyond the hoodie. It's hard to make out his features and I curse the lack of moon tonight. His free hand dusts along the side of my shirt and over to the waistband of my pajama pants.

His touch is tender, featherlight.

He runs his fingers along the sliver of skin that shows

between the two garments. "I've been hard all day thinking about you."

His voice is gravely, and my eyes widen as he shifts his hips, letting me feel the evidence of his confession. Adjusting his position above me, he leans closer to my ear. His breath is hot against my cheek and with just the small change in proximity, I feel myself grow wet between my legs, my body reacting to his presence.

"You're so fucking sexy I nearly came in my pants at the sight of you earlier. All day, I've been thinking about how you'd taste. The sounds you'd make if you let me draw them out of you. I couldn't resist..."

It's *him*.

There's no doubt in my mind he's who was watching me from the roof earlier today. Or was it yesterday? It's not like I can reach for my phone and check the time.

Swallowing thickly, I wait for his next move. My heart hammers within my rib cage as terror clenches me tightly.

"I'm going to take my hand away from your mouth, but if you scream, I'll gag you. Do you understand?"

With him closer, I can make out the intense lightness of his eyes, so crystal blue that his irises look fake. My heart seizes up, not knowing his intentions, yet I feel myself nod beneath his grasp.

As promised, his hand slowly slides away from my mouth and comes to rest around my throat, and he holds it with the same amount of pressure as he did my mouth.

"Who are you?" I croak, my voice coming out strained and distorted. I clear my throat, not even sure why I'm asking when I already know it's him, but I need to hear it.

"Ah, Little Devil. You don't remember me? You put on quite a show earlier...did you think I wouldn't come back?"

I'm frozen on my bed. He's sitting back on his heels now, still straddling my hips but not putting his full weight down. From between his legs, he leans forward slightly to continue holding me in place by my neck while his other hand still ghosts my midriff.

With my eyes fully adjusted, I can see him better. His hoodie is a dark gray, or maybe a worn black. Unzipped halfway, his bare chest is exposed. He's muscular, so damn muscular, and I want to reach up and trace the outline of his pecs with my fingertip.

"How did you get in here?" The words tumble from my lips in a timid stutter.

He laughs and presses his body forward against mine, leaning back down to my ear. "Do you want me to leave?" he whispers.

Shivering, I swallow past the lump in my throat. Despite the terror I feel, I give the slightest shake of my head.

"Because earlier," he continues, "it sure seemed like you wanted me to come down off that roof and eat your pussy. Or were you hoping I'd fuck you instead?"

Pushing his hand into my pants, he brushes his fingers over the fabric of my panties. My hips buck against his touch and he smiles.

Softly, he dusts his lips against my neck, groaning into

it. "Did you dirty your panties with your cum, thinking of me earlier?" His finger grazes lower, and he pushes it into me slightly, still covered with my underwear.

My back arches as I moan. I still haven't answered him. I haven't said a word.

Pushing my hips forward again, I chase his touch when I should be trying to fight him off, trying to get away from him.

His fingers flex against my neck.

"No," I tell him. "The fantasy wasn't enough."

A wide grin spreads across his face, and I marvel at how ruggedly handsome he is. His eyes so bright and vibrant they glow, his five o'clock shadow adding to his features and somehow enhancing his straight jawline more.

"Of course it wasn't. But it's okay, baby girl. I'm here now. And I can feel how much this pussy wants me." He pushes aside the fabric with his middle finger and dips it inside of me. "So perfectly wet, and tight as fuck."

I barely exhale and he's sitting up again, moving the hand that's wrapped around my neck and ripping open my sleep shirt, letting it fall to the side so my breasts are bare. My nipples are already puckered but when the cool air hits them, they harden almost painfully.

"Fuck," he groans and kneads my breast roughly. He grabs it so hard it feels like he's trying to rip it from my body, but he soothes the discomfort by leaning forward and taking my nipple into his mouth.

I suck a breath sharply before it turns into a moan. The

pad of his tongue laps at my breast, and he grabs it roughly with his hand again.

"What is your name?" I half whimper, half moan. He releases my breast with both his hands and mouth, and begins pushing my sleep pants down. His eyes stare into mine as he tugs everything down my legs, panties included.

My subconscious screams at me to tell him to stop— that this is *wrong*—but I don't. I can't. I'm too invested, too turned on, and I would be lying to myself if I said I didn't want this.

But the fact he hasn't even asked if I wanted this sends alarm bells off in my head.

Still, I do nothing, and as he tosses my clothes to the side, I let my legs fall open.

He sits back on his heels again and stares at my pussy with a look of raw desperation in his eyes before turning his gaze to mine. "We don't need to exchange names, baby girl. For only one night, you're mine, and I'm yours. I'll leave before morning and you'll never see me again, but for tonight, I'm going to fulfill your every fantasy. Would you like that?"

# CHAPTER FIVE

H is words echo through my mind.

*I'm going to fulfill your every fantasy. Would you like that?*

This is the craziest, most reckless thing I've ever considered doing. I don't know this man. He literally broke into my house. Yet, I let him undress me. Touch me. I'm considering letting him fuck me.

Would I like that?

"Yes," I tell him, my stare never wavering.

"Only one night," he reiterates.

My head nods, but I don't feel like I'm the one controlling it. Swallowing down the lump that's built in my throat, I repeat, "Only one night."

A wicked smile crawls across his face, and he slowly unzips the hoodie he's wearing and shrugs it off.

Lifting onto my elbows, I prop myself to get a better look at him. My heart skips when I take him in, now that he's removed the hood. If I could describe the ideal man, he'd come damn close. I want to know his name so badly my blood burns, but I bite my tongue and resist asking him again, knowing it's useless.

*Only one night.*

I'd need to keep reminding myself of that.

It wasn't that I haven't had one-night stands. I've had exactly two, thank you very much. But something about this man tells me I'll be craving him for many nights to come.

And I'll never have him again.

I need to remember that, and enjoy whatever tonight will bring.

There's a slight glimmer in his eye that tells me he's thinking the same, or at least I hope he is. He's looking at me like he's trying not to get attached. Reminding himself that whatever this is about to be is just sex.

The moment is fleeting, though, because within an instant the glimmer is gone and replaced with bad intentions. Leaning forward, he slides three of his fingertips against me, testing my wetness.

He smiles again and my heart flutters. As he adjusts himself to lie on his stomach on my bed, he says, "I hope you enjoy Halloween, Little Devil. Because I'm about to make you scream."

I laugh because that's one of the corniest things I've ever heard, but the sound barely passes my lips before his hot mouth is on me and my eyes roll into the back of my head.

He groans, and the vibration spikes through my clit as he attacks it with his tongue. Rough, quick movements roll my clit around, and I squirm beneath him.

Situating on his knees, he leans his forearm against my hips and pins me in place. He brings his other hand up to join his tongue and buries two of his fingers deep in my pussy.

"Oh my *god*," I moan, pushing my legs down into the bed more, attempting to spread them wider.

He pulls away from me, releasing my clit. Immediately, I feel the emptiness of his mouth. "Baby girl, there is no god. There's only me."

His lips wrap around my clit again and he eats me with ferocity, pumping his fingers in at a rhythm similar to his tongue.

Out of nowhere, my body seizes and I'm flooded with a rush of euphoria as my orgasm rips through me.

Writhing beneath him, my hips buck wildly as I chase the release and ride it out. He moves back to watch, but keeps fingering me deeply as my body comes down from the high.

Removing his fingers, he lifts them and even though the room is still completely dark, I can see my cum coat his fingers. He rubs his thumb against it then brings his hand back down and buries his fingers knuckle deep again, pressing his thumb against my clit.

I'm sensitive and resistant to his touch, but within seconds, my body sparks with arousal as he lazily swirls his thumb against me and slowly strokes me inside. His touch is soft, as though he knows it's exactly what I need at the moment.

It feels good. *Too* good. And somehow I feel another orgasm building quickly again.

My walls tighten around his fingers and he smiles, removing them and wiping the juices against my thighs before pushing them back into me, re-coating them with my cum, and repeating the process. He does this a few times, then lowers his face.

Slowly, he licks the inside of my thigh, dragging his tongue against the mess he just made as he laps it up.

My body is on fire as I watch him.

Once finished, he sits up again and wipes the edge of his mouth with his thumb.

"Want to play a game?" he asks, and I nod before he's even finished his sentence. He moves to the edge of the bed and stands, taking something out of his back pocket as he does. In his hand is a piece of fabric, and as he unfolds it, I see it's a mask.

Tugging it over his head, he positions the mask to fit the lower portion of his face. It covers his neck, mouth, and nose, leaving only his piercing eyes on display as the rest of his face becomes the outline of a skeleton. My heart skips, and he continues. "You have a thirty-second head start to run and hide. When I find you—and make no mistake, I *will* find you—I'm going to bury my cock so deep inside you, you'll be lucky if you can walk come morning."

I don't wait for a countdown.

Jumping from my bed, I take off, running out of my bedroom and down the hall, trying to think quickly of where I can go hide. Nearly tripping as I round the corner, I race to my front door, unlock it, and pull it open. Then I slam it shut, leaving it unlocked.

Moving as quickly and quietly on my feet as possible, I keep moving through my house and sneak into the second bedroom that is just off the kitchen, careful not to touch the half-open door in case he notices, and immediately race into the closet.

## CHAPTER SIX

**M**y antics don't seem to slow him, and I'm barely closing the closet door when I hear his heavy footsteps coming toward the guest room. There's not much in this closet, but I press myself against the cold wall and clasp both hands over my mouth to quiet my breathing.

Bursting with adrenaline, excitement, and even a little fear, my heart beats wildly, though I don't think this man would hurt me. But his delicious promise dances through my mind again, and I feel myself grow slick with another gush of wetness between my thighs.

The door to the guest room creaks open slowly, but the sound of footsteps doesn't follow. I hold my breath, my eyes squeezed shut, and wait for him to enter the room.

But he doesn't.

I'm met with the sounds of my own breathing and silence from the house.

Standing frozen against the wall of the closet, a chill

runs over my naked skin. I swallow thickly and remove my hands from my mouth, running them against my arms as I try to eliminate the goosebumps that surfaced.

Seconds turn to minutes, and there's still no sound, no movement, coming from the house.

Self-doubt and confusion run through me, and for a moment I wonder if he changed his mind and left. I wait a few more minutes, then push open the closet door. As I step back into the guest room, a large hand grips my hip and spins me, slamming me face first into the wall.

A scream tears through my chest.

"I thought I told you not to scream," he growls. At the same time, he wraps his arm around my waist and juts my hips backward, pulling my ass flush against him.

"You scared me," I whine, though my voice lacks conviction. My hips move slightly, sensitivity prickling my body as my bare skin rubs against the fabric that covers him.

I feel him maneuvering against me and realize he's shoving his pants down when his skin presses against mine. Moaning from the delicious feeling, I let my forehead fall against the wall for a moment before I tilt my head to the side to catch a glimpse of him. The white of his skeleton mask is a stark contrast to the deep golden hues of his skin and his piercing blue eyes.

Reaching up, I tug at the mask to pull it down. I want to capture his lips and feel them against my own, but he moves his arm from my waist and bats my hand away before I can.

He adjusts my wrists so that they're pressed together above my head and holds them both with a forceful one-handed grip, pushing them against the wall so the texturing bites into my skin.

"Hands to yourself," he snaps, his tone harsh.

He presses his hips against my ass harder. His cock pushes between my legs, the hard shaft rubbing against me, sliding through my arousal.

Pushing his free hand toward my pussy, he plunges a finger inside me, then adds another. Pumping them a few times, he removes them and pulls the wetness to my clit. My knees buckle as I moan again, but I hardly move with the grip he has on me.

Then he spreads my pussy lips, and without warning, slams his cock inside me.

Hissing sharply, I cry out as pain slices through me with the intrusion and how impossibly full I feel. The combination of his size and the angle has me raking my nails against the wall with an instinct to grab something.

"Goddamn, woman," he groans against my neck, hardly giving me time to adjust before he's pulling his hips back and slamming into me again.

Over and over, he thrusts into me punishingly, grunting as he takes his pleasure.

"Such a fucking good slut, aren't you, Little Devil?" he murmurs against my ear before reaching down and slapping my clit.

The harsh assault makes me cry out again.

"Letting a man you don't even know fuck you like this,"

he continues. "I knew you'd open your legs for me. I could see the way you were about to fuck yourself for me by the pool. Were your panties wet because of the water, or because of how much you wanted your pussy licked, Little Devil?"

My eyes roll back into my head as he positions his fingers against my clit and begins to rub—the motions just as rough as his thrusts.

"Answer me," he hisses, increasing the intensity of his touch.

But I can hardly remember what he asked.

"Wh–what?" I stutter, well aware that my mind is completely useless to me right now. I'm too lost to the pleasure.

"Tell me how bad you wanted to fuck yourself for me."

"I almost did," I breathe. My body begins to ignite, another orgasm tingling through me as I draw closer to it.

He's still fucking me with purpose, unrelenting as he chases his release. The sound of skin slapping skin fills the air and a moment later, he's pounding me so hard, I have to tilt my head backward to keep it from hitting the wall.

"Until my brother came, right, Little Devil?" He slows into a torturous rhythm, taking his time as he pulls himself out until just the tip remains inside me, then pushes in slowly. Over and over. "*Fuck*. I know I said one night, but maybe if you're really lucky, next time it'll be both of us who show up. Then you can show us how you play with this pretty pussy."

I whimper as he rolls my clit between his fingers, and as his words fade away, he resumes the intensity of his thrusts.

With a roar he comes, neither of us caring that his cum is filling me up. Leaning down, he rests his forehead against my shoulder blade, both of us taking a second to catch our breath.

My chest heaves and as he pulls out, I wince slightly, already sore. The moment his cock is gone, some of his cum slides out of me and down my thighs.

Stepping away, he releases his hold on me and I turn around. My breath hitches as I look at the man in front of me, completely naked except for the skeleton mask that covers half his face. His broad chest glistens with a layer of sweat, and his cock, still hard as stone, juts out between his legs. His pants pool around his feet and as he steps out of them my eyes linger on the hand wrapped around his cock as he pumps it slowly.

"Would you like that, Little Devil?" he asks as his hand slides up and down his shaft.

"If your brother watches me?"

He takes a step forward, caging me against the wall again. Bringing his hand to my neck, he presses his hand against my throat and leans in until the fabric of his mask grazes my ear. "We could each pick a hole. Fuck you so hard you won't be able to walk straight for a week."

"You'd fuck me together?" I ask, not completely understanding his suggestion. I read a lot of taboo books, but the idea of it coming to life was another story. "With your *brother*?"

His hand drifts from my neck, down between my breasts, and when he reaches my pussy, he wastes no time pushing two fingers inside of me. As he begins fucking me with his hand, he pulls his mask down, and licks the side of my face. "I think you like the idea. This sweet cunt of yours sure does. Listen to how wet you are."

The movements of his fingers increase and he's right, I can hear it.

"Fuck me again," I beg. Pushing his hand away from me, his eyes flare, then darken, as I push off from the wall.

"Run."

And I do. I sprint from the guest room and across the kitchen, making it halfway down the hall before he catches me by the hair and yanks me back.

Crying out, my hand flies to the base of my skull, where it feels like it's been lit on fire. In a quick movement, he releases the hold and whips his hand around to my neck, grabbing it tightly as he slams me back against his chest. His fingers move up to grip my jaw, and he turns my head toward him.

"Gotcha," he snarls, then he slams his lips against mine.

My mouth opens automatically and his tongue finds mine. The kiss is anything but sweet.

Menacing, rough, bruising.

I feel his other hand sweep down my backside before his fingers are back inside me, thrusting hard.

Moaning, I tilt my ass toward him, spurring him on.

"You're a filthy little slut, aren't you? My cum's still

dripping out of this cunt, and you're already ready for more."

Keeping me tight against his body, we walk toward my bedroom. Once through the threshold, he pushes me forward, catching me off guard.

I stumble to the bed, and before I can turn around, he's shoving me down. Bent at the waist, he pushes the back of my head into my comforter and slams his cock into me from behind.

"Holy shit," I murmur against the soft blanket, shifting my head slightly so I can breathe better.

A searing pain radiates against my skin as his palm connects with my ass.

"It's going to be hard to walk away from you," he growls, and I go still.

As hot as this is, it isn't real. It's a fantasy. One night only, no more. But they're just words. Sex-induced words.

Pulling out of me until only the tip of him is buried inside, he slides back in excruciatingly slow. He repeats his movements, holding onto my hips as his fingernails bite into my skin.

Briefly, I wonder if I'll wake up with bruises and marks in the morning.

I don't hate the idea.

Reaching between my legs, my fingers connect with my clit, and I moan again. The extra stimulation is exactly what I need.

"Does that cunt of yours want to come?" he asks, and I frantically shake my head yes. Because I do. So badly, I need to come again. "Well, too fucking bad," he says, and knocks my hand away from my clit.

I whimper in protest, and he grabs my wrist, yanking it behind me. He holds it against my back as he continues fucking me deeply, once again using my body for his pleasure.

Still, I can feel how wet I am, my cum mixed with his, as he slides in and out.

It feels so good. So out of my comfort zone, but if this is how it feels to be out of it, I never want back in.

Curling my fingers around the blankets on my bed, I close my eyes and let my other senses take over. The sounds of his grunts fill the room. The scent of sex and sweat permeates around us. And the *feeling*. The devastatingly erotic feeling of his cock stretching me—it's all too much to handle. Despite the lack of clitoral stimulation, my heightened senses push me to the brink of orgasm.

I can feel it. So close as a scattering of tingles filters through my bloodstream.

And then it's here.

Crying out, my orgasm rips through me and sends me sky high. My eyes roll back. My toes curl. It's so intense it almost hurts. The only thing I can do is grip the sheets and bite down on the linens beneath me.

He lets me ride the high, continuing his merciless thrusts, but I don't miss the way he groans in pleasure as I drench his cock.

My body trembles as he jerks out of me and flips me over like a rag doll, as though I weigh absolutely nothing.

I'm surprised to see he's readjusted his mask, positioning it back on his face again. His eyes are nearly black as he stares down at me, his gaze penetrating mine with a look that's nearly unreadable. Still, I sit wordlessly, leaning back on my forearms as I catch my breath.

Pulling my gaze, I glance down at my body—at the raw and primal way I'm positioned in front of him. Leaned back, legs spread and bent over the edge of the bed, the mixture of our cum dripping from me. My nipples are painfully erect, my chest heaving.

Wild.

I look and feel absolutely, carnally, wild.

And as I look back at him, the only thing I can think of is how badly I want to rip that skeleton mask from his face completely so I can continue to feel his lips against mine.

# CHAPTER SEVEN

I t's almost as though he can read my thoughts, because his hand lifts and he finally yanks his mask completely off, tossing it down onto the bed next to me.

"Let's go, Little Devil," he growls in my ear as he leans down next to it. His fingertips trail against my thigh and dip into the heat between my legs, and I moan, dropping my head backward as my eyes close.

As his fingers pump inside me, his other hand wraps around my hair, tugging my head back even further. With the arch of my neck exposed, he licks up the column as he fingers me, stopping just below my jaw.

The sensation sends a shiver down my spine. But as quickly as the shiver passes, he's yanking me up by my hair and pulling me to my feet.

His grasp is firm, his fist pressed against my scalp, as he guides me through my house until we're at my back slider.

"Where are we going?" I yelp as the frigid night air hits

my face. He's pulling me toward the pool, and my eyes widen. "Nope, no. Not going in there, it's freezing!"

He grunts in response as we stop at the edge and releases my hair. "You had no problem getting in there earlier today and giving me a show. Time to recreate it for me."

"I'm not going in there. It was freezing earlier today, and that was when the sun was out!"

"Oh, c'mon, it'll be fun," he says, giving me a wicked smile.

Then he reaches out and pushes me into the pool.

Coldness overtakes me, sending an icy cascade across my naked body the second I'm underwater. Kicking my legs, I fight against the unwelcoming chokehold the temperature has over me, but before I make it to the surface, the water is disturbed again. Bubbles erupt around me as the telltale sound of another body jumping in collides with the water, and arms wrap around me.

With another set of legs kicking, we're instantly above the water nearing the shallow end, and I'm gasping for air.

Warm lips begin kissing my neck as I grip the side of the pool as I stand on my tiptoes, and turn to look at him.

"What the hell was that?" I seethe.

But he merely chuckles and cages me against the siding. His tongue finds its way into my mouth as he kisses me with abandon. Our tongues dance together wildly and although I mentally curse myself for doing so, I wrap my arms around his neck and pull him closer.

Sliding his hand between my legs, he picks up where he

left off earlier and slips his fingers back inside of me. As his thumb rubs against my clit, I buck my hips and chase his touch.

"I always get what I want, Little Devil," he says against my lips. "And what I want is to recreate what I saw earlier."

Taking a step backward in the water, his hands grip my hips and he lifts me. Water cascades down my body as he sets me down on the edge. My feet dangle in the water, and I shiver. His voice is gruff, thick with arousal as he says, "Lay back and play with your pussy for me."

Goosebumps pebble my entire body from the clash of the water and night air, but I do as he says and lay back against the concrete. Placing my feet on the edge of the pool, I situate myself as comfortably as I can, and slide my hand down my body.

Naturally, my fingers find my clit and I begin to rub myself in lazy circles, watching him from between my bent legs.

His eyes flare from where he watches in the water, and he fixates on the movement. "Push your finger in. See how drenched you are from my cum filling you."

Tilting my wrist further, my finger dips into my heat, sliding in as deep as I can from this angle. The heel of my hand pushes against my sensitive clit, the sensation causing my hips to lift. A heady moan floats past my lips.

"Feel good, baby girl?" he asks as he pushes his palms against the edge of the pool and lifts himself, settling on his forearms so he's between my legs. The water sways around him as his feet and lower legs remain in the water.

My mind is like jelly, complete mush, and I'm unable to form a coherent thought. The best I can do is hum my agreement with a soft "Mmm."

Continuing my ministrations, I slowly finger myself, adding another to increase the pleasure. His warm breath skates across my pussy as he lowers his mouth closer.

Bringing his finger between my legs, he dips it below where mine is pushed inside me and plays with the cum escaping, pulling it down to the part of my body no man has ever entered. I flinch when his finger breaches the hole, pushing in softer than I imagined he would and testing the first ring of muscles.

He surprises me when he doesn't push further than that, but instead removes both of our hands and replaces it with his tongue. Prodding my slit, he laps at the juices and suctions around my clit as he slides both hands beneath my ass and grips my cheeks tightly, holding me in place while I ride his face.

Groaning, he matches the swipes of his tongue to the way I lift my hips, drawing out my continuous moans until my entire body clenches and vibrates with an intense orgasm.

Before I've even finished trembling, he's completely out of the pool and crawling up my body until his hips are positioned over my shoulders. With his cock in hand, he rubs the tip against my lips, coating them with his pre-cum. He says nothing and leans his body forward, pushing his cock to coax my lips to open and surround his shaft.

He easily slides down my throat, making me gag

slightly, as he shifts his position to lean on his forearms again, giving him the stability to thrust into my mouth. And I let him fuck my mouth as I fight against my instinct to gag.

Tears stream down my face as he seeks pleasure, and I hollow my cheeks, grabbing onto the backs of his thighs until his hot cum slides down my throat and he groans in bliss.

His movements slow, and he slides from me, settling back on his heels as he looks down at me with a smile on his face. Reaching up, he swipes his thumbs against my cheeks and wipes the messy tears, then slides his fingertips down the column of my neck.

"Did I hurt you?" he asks, watching his hand as it glides down my body and leaves goosebumps in its wake.

"No," I whisper into the night. "That was amazing."

And I mean it. A big part of me wants to pull him back down to suck him off again.

With his hand on my hip, he gives it a tight squeeze before reaching around behind him, finding my pussy. "You're *still* wet and dripping for me, Little Devil."

The grin on his face is mischievous as he pushes two fingers inside me, even from the awkward angle he sits at.

I'm sore and sensitive, but his touch sets my skin on fire and I'm instantly writhing beneath him again. My voice sounds foreign to my ears when I whisper, "Fuck me again, *please*."

"Such a greedy little slut, so hungry for my dick, aren't you?"

My head nods, the back of my skull digging into the rough concrete as I agree with him.

"Alright then, let's see how many times I can fuck you before you pass out, Little Devil." Scurrying to his feet, he extends his hand and I reach for it, letting him pull me to a stand.

As soon as I'm in his arms, his lips connect with mine again and his fingers find my clit, making my knees buckle. His strong arms hold me up as I whimper from his unforgiving touch.

"Fuck, you're addicting," he groans and reaches down to my thighs, lifting me and coaxing my legs to wrap around him.

Gripping my ass tightly, he carries me inside and back to my bedroom, whispering filthy promises in my ear as he walks us through my house.

## CHAPTER EIGHT

When I wake the next morning, it's unsurprising that he's already gone. My thoughts trickle back to last night. Flashes of him from behind me. The brutal way he'd grab me. The merciless way he fucked me. The way my body bent and conformed to his every desire as he used it over and over.

Tingles bloom at the mere recollection, and I press my thighs together under the blankets to ease the pressure already building.

Something isn't right though, and as I lift the blanket from my body, I realize I'm wearing my pajamas.

The same pajamas that were ripped from my body last night.

The pajamas that should be laying ruined on the floor.

Pushing my legs over the edge of my bed, I sit up and look around at the way my bed is pristine on one side; the pillows aligned perfectly with the other half of my duvet covering them part way.

Rubbing my hand down my face, I stand and try to figure out what's going on.

Did he make the bed before he left? Cleaned up before sneaking away?

Slowly, I move through my house, trying to shake the eerie feeling harbored in my chest. Maybe he's still here?

"Hello?" I stop moving and listen, but am met with silence.

Moving toward my kitchen, my eyes catch on the guest room door that sits halfway open.

Odd, since I remember it being wide open after we moved from the space last night.

A curious need claws at me, urging me to step into the room and check the closet door, but I refrain, if only for a moment.

Pushing the door open, the room comes into view, as does the closet.

The closet door is closed.

My hand flutters to my collarbone and I run my finger across it rhythmically, like I do when my anxiety starts to appear. The motion soothes me as I force myself to think logically.

But all sense of logic has flown out the window.

The doors to both the guest room and the guest room's closet should be open. Not closed.

And my bed was *destroyed* last night. With blankets falling to the floor, the sheet barely pulled across the mattress. I fell asleep in a sex-induced haze in my messy bed. With *him* by my side, his arm laying across my stomach. Both naked and satiated.

Right?

Walking back into my bathroom, I stare at myself in the mirror, studying my reflection. Mascara has smeared slightly under my eyes from sleeping with my makeup on, and my hair doesn't appear as messy as I thought it would after the events of last night. My eyes don't look sleep deprived, nor do my lips look puffy as they would after being thoroughly kissed and using my mouth in various other ways through the night.

My breathing hitches.

I don't feel sore, either. The sweet ache between my legs that should be there isn't.

Without another thought, I rip my sleep pants and underwear down until they reach mid-thigh and look down at them.

They're dry, when there should be at least some evidence of last night's salaciousness.

But there's just...nothing.

Pushing the fabrics further down, I let them pool at my feet as I undo the buttons of my sleep shirt.

*The buttons.*

*He ripped my shirt off last night.*

My fingers begin to tremble as I look down at the buttons that are very much still attached to the shirt and looped through their respective holes.

A whimper catches in my throat, my blood running cold.

*What the hell is going on?*

Walking into my walk-in closet, I dress quickly in jeans and a floral t-shirt, pushing my feet into the sandals that sit neatly by the closet. My mind is a hazy mess of self-doubt and confusion as I make my way through my house and out my front door.

The breeze is chilly, and I wrap my arms around myself while I walk to my neighbor's house. A bowl of Halloween candy sits untouched next to her front door.

"Mrs. Johnson?" I shout while knocking persistently, knowing she wears hearing aids and might not hear me right away. "Mrs. Johnson, are you home?"

I catch myself looking left to right, keeping an eye on my surroundings. It feels like I'm being watched, though my mind might be playing tricks on me.

Seconds feel like minutes as I wait for her to answer the door, and a whoosh of relief runs through me once she finally does.

"Good morning, my dear! How have you been?"

Forcing myself to not show my panic outwardly, I smile as sweetly as I can muster. "I'm doing well, thank you so much."

And then I'm at a loss for words.

Why am I here? What exactly do I hope to achieve by knocking on this woman's door first thing in the morning?

But I need answers. I need to know that I'm not crazy,

because right now I feel like I'm going completely out of my mind.

"I couldn't help but notice that you had workers on your roof yesterday!" I exclaim a little too cheerfully. I try to rein it in. "Since I'm still pretty new to the area, I am trying to compile a list of service providers that the neighbors use for if I ever have anything go wrong at my place."

I guess it wasn't a complete lie; still, I hate being deceitful.

"Workers, dear?" she questions, and the look on her face tells me she truly is confused.

"Yeah," I drawl, hesitating slightly. "The two men on your roof around three o'clock yesterday?"

Her lips purse, and my stomach plummets.

"You must be mistaken. I haven't had workers around the house in months."

"You...what? There were no men working here yesterday?"

"Not a single one. It's a shame, too. I should break something so I can get a strapping young handyman to fix it for me." She grins, but I can't bring myself to return it.

"So, you didn't have anyone here doing something on top of your roof? A contractor? Roofers? Chimney sweepers?" Panic bubbles in my throat and I swallow it down, careful not to break the calm mask I'm wearing and frighten the old woman.

My mind drifts to the image of his skeleton mask.

She shakes her head. "You must be confused with a different house?"

I'm not, but I don't tell her that. The echo of my heart is hammering in my ears as a wave of nausea hits me.

"You look a little green, dear. Are you feeling okay?" she asks, but I'm already halfway down her stairs, running back toward my house.

How is this possible? What is going on?

He was there. On her roof. I *saw* him. He broke into my house last night. Fucked me six ways to Sunday.

Right?

Tears prickle my eyes as I rip open my front door and slam it behind me once I'm inside. I'm frozen in place, leaning against the door with my hand over my mouth as I think back to everything I know.

There was a man on the roof when I surfaced from the pool.

He watched me, then he left.

I ate dinner last night, turned on a movie, and went to bed.

He broke into my house and then made me come again and again.

We went to sleep.

I woke up alone.

Sinking to the floor, I bring my knees to my chest and wrap my arms around my legs, continuing to think and process everything.

So many things don't add up.

We went to sleep in my messy, destroyed bed, yet when I woke up, the bed was practically made, and pristine on one side.

I fell asleep naked, but when I woke up, my clothes were in their original condition, not ripped and removed as they should have been.

Though we had sex multiple times—*unprotected* sex—and I should have had a huge mess between my legs, I don't.

No bruises on my body. My hair is not as unruly as to be expected.

Doors and rooms were untouched, the house still locked up.

*Nothing* looks like it should after the events of the night.

*Only one night.*

Only the craziest, most out of my comfort zone, yet blissfully fan-fucking-tastic night of my life.

Yet, I have no proof.

And I'm going to go out of my mind trying to figure out what is happening.

# CHAPTER NINE

The day flew by, but throughout the duration I simultaneously felt like I was in a state of pause and fast forward, as though the two concepts could work together. I can't remember a single thing I did, my mind ensnared by confusion.

Nothing makes sense.

Going through the motions of cooking dinner, I turn on the TV again for some background noise, settling, for some reason I can't comprehend, on the evening news.

I never watch the evening news. It's depressing and boring, and frankly, the alerts that come through on my cell phone are plenty. But tonight, after a day of convincing myself that I'm crazy, I turn it on. Maybe a dose of reality will help me work through this.

Scooping spaghetti into my white ceramic bowl, I mentally question why I made spaghetti, anyway. Yet again,

I made enough to feed a party of ten, like I always do. I can never just make a little, it's always a lot.

*"Reports of many neighborhood houses being T.P.'d last night have come in, and residents of this sleepy community are wondering if they were targeted by a group of unruly trick-or-treaters."*

My eyes roll as I shake grated parmesan over the top of my dinner, adding practically half the container. Shoveling a big bite into my mouth, I lift my eyes to the screen to see the camera crew span an entire street of homes whose front landscapes and porches are covered in toilet paper.

*"While most homeowners think this is an act of years-old pranking, some aren't so sure."*

*"I've lived in this neighborhood for thirty years and have never had my house vandalized like it was last night. Who's going to clean this up? Not me, that's who. The parents of these delinquents should be held responsible!"*

I shake my head at the man's words. Now I understand why there are fifty-five and over communities.

It was Halloween last night—what does he expect?

Swallowing my last bite, I stand from where I'm bent over the kitchen island and move toward the sink, placing my bowl down gently as I turn on the faucet and let the stream of water turn to hot.

Over the water, I hear the news switch reporters and glance back at the TV. The young male anchor stands in front of a home, holding his microphone with both hands. He introduces himself and begins talking about a string of home burglaries around town.

Once the sponge is full of soapsuds and the water is hot, I scrub my bowl, trying to get the sauce off before it stains.

*"The pattern prior to the burglaries appears to be the same, as eyewitnesses recount seeing two men on top of their neighbors' roofs days earlier—"*

I whip my body around so quickly, soapy water sloshes from the bowl and onto the floor.

*"Police have worked with forensic artists to create sketches of what they believe these men may look like—"*

All the air siphons from the room when the screen switches to a police sketch of the man from the roof—my man from the roof. The resemblance is uncanny, almost identical to how he really looks, and as the screen switches to the sketch of the other man—the man I assume is the brother he spoke of—I nearly choke on the sob that catches in my throat.

*"It's believed these two men are brothers who may be connected to the string burglaries in neighboring towns. Police are encouraging the public to stay vigilant and to reach out to local law enforcement immediately if you have any information. This is Bennett Radcliff, signing off with News Now Channel One."*

Thoughts ricochet through my mind faster than a bullet and I spin myself back toward the sink just as the news goes to commercial break. With the bowl in one hand, I brace my other against the edge of the sink and stare blankly into the empty basin.

It's him.

*I wasn't going crazy.*

A wave of nausea hits me as I white knuckle where the countertop meets the sink.

*Burglaries. He's connected to a string of burglaries.*

Allegedly.

*Maybe it's not true.*

My thoughts filter back to waking up with him on top of me, his hand covering my mouth.

*He broke in.*

I swallow down the bitter reality and turn the faucet back on to finish washing my dishes. At this moment, I need to force myself to focus on the task at hand instead of completely breaking down like I want to. The pit at the bottom of my stomach is growing by the second, and I can feel the tears rushing to prick the backs of my eyes.

With my breaths growing labored from anxiety, I pick up the sponge and wash my bowl to its entirety before placing it back down and blowing out a shaky breath.

As I do, my eyes catch on something outside of the window over the sink, and I can't help but release my grasp on the bowl as my hand flies over my mouth to suppress a scream. Ceramic shattering clashes against the commercial playing on the TV that suddenly sounds too loud.

There he is, leaning against the pole of the streetlight as if he doesn't have a single care in the world. With his arms crossed over his chest and a smirk on his painfully handsome face, he stands there in a fitted jacket, t-shirt, and jeans, looking far too good for an alleged criminal.

For several seconds, all I can do is stare back in disbelief, trying to get control of the emotions I'm feeling inside. Fear, confusion, arousal—everything conflicts and weighs heavy.

Glancing down at the shattered bowl, I turn off the stream of water that's been continuously running and grab the dish towel to wipe my hands. The fabric is soft against my skin and gives a fleeting sense of comfort.

Seconds later, I look up again, and he's gone.

Standing on my tiptoes, I lean against the sink and peer out the window, looking for him, before I turn and run to my front door. I'm through it and in my front yard faster than I can comprehend, and suddenly enveloped by the cold autumn air.

Wrapping my hands around my middle, I'm suddenly all too aware that I'm jacketless and barefoot. Still, I search for him, making a complete three-hundred and sixty degree turn, but he's nowhere.

He's just...gone.

The street is silent, not even the crickets are out, and the gentle *whoosh* of the light wind breezes through the trees, swaying their branches in a slow dance.

There are no footsteps. No shadows cast.

Gone.

My feet carry me to each side of my front yard as I check the side gates, both of which are locked. The fences are too high for someone to jump over, although I probably shouldn't underestimate someone the police are looking for in regards to home burglaries.

Back in my house, I make sure my front door is locked

before I cross the width and unlock my slider, stepping back out into the cold air.

This time, I shove my feet into the flip-flops I leave by my back door.

My eyes scan the open yard, and back through the view-fence, and I'm met with nothing.

A strong gust pulsates around me, and I shiver before turning back to go inside.

And just like that, I'm confused all over again.

Lowering myself onto the couch, I sit and stare into my lap, trying to process and go through each and every *fact* I can think of.

Because the thought of this all being fiction scares me.

The idea that I've made this all up in my head and now my mind is playing hyper-realistic tricks on me is terrifying.

Once my breathing evens out again, and the tears stop burning my eyes, I pick myself up and go through the motions for the rest of the evening. Mechanically, I pick up the broken pieces from the bowl that shattered, finish cleaning up the leftovers, and leave the pot to soak overnight. I shower, blow-dry my hair, and get into my most comfortable pajamas before pouring myself a glass of wine and curl into the comfort of my bed.

And then I try to let my mind go numb.

# CHAPTER TEN

The bright rays of the sun shining through the curtains stir me awake. Reaching my arms out, I stretch lazily with my eyes still clamped shut, and expel a yawn. My arms dip to my left, and I'm caught off guard when I bump into a cushion. Confused, I look and realize I'm on the couch.

Sitting up quickly, my feet touch the floor as I take in my living room. The TV is on, a random early morning show playing. On the table in front of me sits a dirty bowl and fork.

My body prickles with awareness and I stand, turning to look around. There's a stillness that surrounds me, as it does every morning. Living alone is vastly different from living with a spouse. And although I relish the silence, I still haven't quite gotten used to the quiet mornings and the solitude of not sharing a space with another person.

Memories from the the last day and a half are fuzzy at

best, and I'm confused as hell, rubbing my temples and trying to remember all the details.

Everything looks as it should, but I can't shake the feeling of something being off. Still, I don't understand how I ended up on the couch, wearing yoga pants and a t-shirt...

I gasp and fall back onto the couch as bits and pieces slam into me. The pool, the man, the sex, my neighbor's confusion...the news report. Tears flood my eyes as my heart increases with intense palpitations sputtering in my chest.

Reaching for my phone off the coffee table, it illuminates as I pick it up, showing me the time and date.

When I see the date, I lose it.

Tears stream down my face as my eyes transfix on the month and day.

November first.

The day after Halloween.

*Impossible. It's the second. How did I lose an entire day?*

What the fuck is going on?

Slamming my eyes shut, I rub them roughly with my knuckles and look again.

There has to be a glitch with my phone. Stupid technology.

Rushing outside, the autumn sun assaults my eyes as I go to the edge of my driveway and pick up the newspaper that's left there every morning.

The one I throw away every afternoon.

Ripping the plastic off it, I flick the paper open and

look at the date in the corner.

November first.

Nausea pummels through me, bile rising in my throat. It has to be wrong.

"Good mornin'!" my neighbor across the street calls, and I realize he's the answer to my prayers.

Shoving my nerves aside, I reach my hand upward in a wave. "Morning, Mr. Hale. What a beautiful November morning! How was your Halloween?"

He doesn't hesitate to chuckle and walk to the edge of his driveway. "Last night was uneventful, as usual. No trick or treaters, and Lydia and I were in bed by eight. How about yours?"

If it was even possible, I physically felt the color drain from my face. Mr. Hale must have noticed it too, because he added, "Hon, are you feeling okay? You look like you've seen a ghost."

Had I?

Seen a ghost? Or was it all just an intensely vivid dream?

"You know what, I'm not feeling the greatest and need to go lie down. Have a nice day, Mr. Hale." And then I turn away.

My feet only carry me to my couch, where I emotionlessly sit down and put my head in my hands.

Nothing makes sense, and now my head is beginning to throb with a headache.

Throughout my divorce, my ex-husband called me crazy on more than one occasion. Maybe he was right, because right now I certainly *feel* crazy.

Laying down, I curl into myself on my couch and stare blankly at whatever is on the TV and watch the scenes change.

Nothing registers—the dialogue, the music—it's all just background to the jumbled mess in my brain. Little bits of Halloween night flicker through my mind, but there's not a single thing I can pinpoint to be factual.

The only thing I can conclude is that it was a dream.

It was a *dream*.

A wild, vivid, sexual fantasy my mind made up after seeing that man on my neighbor's roof.

So why did it *feel* so damn real? Why can't I shake the feeling that it had happened?

I replay everything I can remember over and over, picking it apart and analyzing it. My thoughts begin to spiral, ideas and theories spinning a web in my brain.

The only thing that's clear to me is that I need to check my house. I need to investigate every room I remember being in, go outside by the pool...anything that might help jog my memory more.

When I get up from the couch, I notice from the window that the sky has changed into deep hues of oranges and reds. Checking my phone again, I'm awestruck to see that I've spent the entire day on my couch.

On cue, my stomach rumbles with hunger, but I ignore it.

I go from room to room, but nothing is out of place. Everything looks exactly how it should, down to the lines on the guestroom carpet from when I vacuumed a few days ago.

"*It was a dream,*" I tell myself firmly. "*There's no other explanation. You had a vivid dream that felt incredibly real, but that's all it was. A dream.*"

Sinking onto the edge of the guest bed, I tell myself that it was a dream over and over again, until I start to believe it.

And I do, because there's no other explanation. It. Was. A. Dream.

It was a dream.

By the time I step into my kitchen to make something to eat, my hands are trembling, but I force myself to focus on the task at hand. Pulling out some vegetables from the crisper drawer, I line them up by the sink and return to the refrigerator for the package of chicken waiting to be cooked.

As I preheat the oven, I prep the chicken first, tossing it in olive oil, seasonings, and minced garlic, before placing it in a glass baking dish and setting it on the counter by the stove. It's then that I realize it's too quiet in the house and tell my Alexa to play music. She turns on a mix perfectly curated to what I like, and I start singing along as I turn to wash the veggies.

When they're ready to be chopped, I take them to the kitchen island and reach for my favorite knife. As I remove it from the butcher block, my eyes catch on a single folded piece of paper sitting on the floor under the mail slot in my front door.

Something in my gut tells me it's the answer to a thousand questions, yet I don't know how it could be. Still, I abandon the vegetables and walk over to pick it up.

Unfolding it, the breath catches in my throat as I read what it says. The handwriting is sloppy, but legible.

*Next time it'll be both of us.*

I flip the paper over, but it's blank on the other side. Next time it'll be both of us? What does that even mean? Both of *who*?

I try to think, but I come up short.

Shaking my head, I return to the kitchen and wash my hands, turning back to the vegetables once more and continue to chop them.

As I work on the second to last bell pepper, a memory slams into me.

*"I know I said one night, but maybe if you're really lucky, next time it'll be both of us who show up. Then you can show us how you play with this pretty pussy."*

The knife falls with a clatter to the marble countertop and I sink to my knees on the floor, more confused than ever, and try to stop myself from hyperventilating.

My thoughts spiral as I try to connect the dots and decide what is real. Squeezing my eyes shut, I recite the sentence I've been repeating all night, trying to believe my own words.

*It was a dream.*

It was a dream.

It. Was. A. Dream.

But then again, maybe it wasn't.

# ACKNOWLEDGMENTS

I hope you enjoyed this short, spicy read! Thank you so much to all of my amazing readers who have taken a chance on my books. Without you, writing would still just be a dream I was too scared to chase. Your support and willingness to read my words means the world to me.

A very special thank you to my amazing team! My alpha and beta readers who really help shape the story: Amanda, DeLynda, Tawny, Kerri & Megan. Thank you to my editorial team, Virginia Carey and Nicole Bucciarelli.

To my husband, parents, and my besties Amanda, April, for always being there for me throughout my writing journey, and for being the best cheerleaders I could ever ask for.

An extra special thank you to the amazing teams of women I have on my promo squad and my ARC team, and the influencers who always show their love and support. And of course to my PA, Cassie, who I truly don't think I could live without! I'm so grateful for you and all that you've helped me accomplish so far.

LOVE YOU ALL.

A.R. Rose is a wife, mom, reader, and writer, who lives in sunny California with her family and doggo. She loves to hang out at home, drink copious amounts of coffee, and eat yummy food

90% of the time you will find her with a book or her Kindle in hand, reading a spicy romance novel, which not so coincidentally is what she has fallen in love with writing.

# CONNECT

**Join A.R. Rose's newsletter for info & updates**
 ♥https://www.authorarrose.com/email-subscribe

**Website**
 ♥www.authorarrose.com

**Reading Group**
 ♥https://www.facebook.com/groups/authorarrose

**Facebook**
 ♥https://www.facebook.com/authorarrose

**TikTok**
 ♥https://www.tiktok.com/@authorarrose

**Instagram**
 ♥ https://www.instagram.com/authorarrose

Need more A.R. Rose?

Continue reading for a peek of an ex-boyfriend's brother,
Motorcycle club romance, that'll keep you on the edge of
your seat!

# A.R. ROSE

🏍 Ex-boyfriend's brother
🏍 Small Town
🏍 Motorcycle Club
🏍 Redemption
🏍 Second Chance
🏍 He Falls First

# CHAPTER ONE

*Rosie*

*Six Years Ago*

"I'm not sure what you're not comprehending, Rosie. You either get a fucking job and throw down on a portion of the rent, or you find somewhere else to stay. It's not like you're doing anything else to help us with this fucking house." Brent slammed the dresser drawer shut, smashing the arm of a t-shirt as he did. My boyfriend was such an asshole—so hot and cold about literally everything.

*"You can stay here as long as you need, babe."*

*"Don't worry about rent, babe. Focus on finding a job."*

My plan was never to stay here permanently, but I needed more time to get on my feet. I just moved here because of him. We weren't serious enough to move in together, but a fresh start sounded like exactly what I needed, so I figured, why not? I'd get a studio, find a job, screw my boyfriend.

Life would be easy.

Except it wasn't. Finding a job was proving to be a little more difficult than I had initially thought, but it was fine. I just needed to lower my standards of where I was applying.

Once I did, I had three interviews lined up. One of them was bound to hire me. *Hopefully*.

The grocery store would, no doubt. Who got turned away by a grocery store?

It'd been two months, and I didn't want to be in Brent's bed every night any more than he wanted me in it. We had a very... relaxed relationship. And by relaxed I mean, we played the part of boyfriend/girlfriend when we felt like it but weren't so serious that we were discussing solid plans about our future.

And before you go chastising me and thinking, *'but Rosie, you moved for him'*, just remember, I moved for *me*. He just happened to present me with a place to stay and a crutch to lean against as I got settled.

Brent and I were not headed toward Mr. and Mrs., that was for damn sure.

Sounds awful, right? I did love Brent. I just didn't see us growing old together. He was my right now, not my forever. There was a difference.

"Why would I help with the house when I'm not the one who makes the mess? I keep my shit clean. It's really not that hard, Brent. You and your brother should figure out how to do the same."

"You're such a fucking bitch sometimes, you know that,

right? I think I've been more than fair to you, Rosie, and I'm done with you and your games."

I rolled my eyes and glanced down at my black-painted nails in boredom. "Yeah, yeah, Brent. Done with me until tonight, when you beg me to spread my legs."

"I don't beg for shit."

"Keep telling yourself that. I'll keep them closed for a while and we'll see how long you can hold out for."

"You think I won't go elsewhere?"

"Don't care."

"We'll see how much you don't care later when I make your ass sleep on the couch and you have to listen to me pound into someone else through these paper-thin walls."

"Go for it. I'll just crawl into your brother's bed," I spat, my heart skipping a beat at the very thought of it.

See, while I may have met Brent first, it was hard to deny the attraction I had for his brother.

Brent was your classic all-star, preppy, clean-cut, boy-next-door. The type who was the perfect person to bring home to your parents and start making lifelong plans with.

On the outside.

On the *inside*, he could be a real-fucking jerk. Like, want to scratch his eyes out and punch him in the nuts, kind of jerk.

It was baffling how he'd somehow wormed his way inside of my heart.

We'd been together for over a year now, if you don't count the month we were broken up. I *did* care about him. Honestly, what we had worked for us. And when he wasn't being a raging dickwad, Brent was actually very sweet and attentive. We had fun together. High highs. Low lows.

Toxic, I know. What I just described was practically the definition of a walking red flag.

But again, it worked for us. It worked for *now*.

Brent was a few years older than me, and the type of relationship he wanted was one of convenience and fun. It was a relationship I knew I could easily give him, because in return he could give me the sense of stability I craved. I was a little wild, I knew it and owned it, and I needed a person in my life to ground me—balance me out. Most of the time, he gave me that.

It also didn't help that Brent was pretty damn hot. But while he had the boy-next-door vibe, his brother was his polar opposite...the bad boy. Two years younger, rough around the edges, and devastatingly, ruggedly, gorgeous. Even his name was as sinful as he was—*Cain*.

He was covered in tattoos—which really matched my energy—and he didn't give a fuck about anything or anyone.

Actually, the only thing he did give a fuck about was Brent.

And *me*.

Which was a real bitch since I was technically with his brother.

Cain and I just connected better than Brent and I did, though we never crossed *that* line. But man, if you could actually fuck someone with your eyes, there wouldn't be a time or a place he hadn't taken me. Many late nights were spent in each other's company, talking about anything you could imagine. Our guards had come fully down, and I honestly wasn't sure anyone knew me better than he did. So many times I'd thought about telling Brent we were finished. I was hopeful I could leave him and one day move forward and be with Cain.

But Cain was never willing to let it happen.

Because I was his brother's girlfriend, I was off-limits completely. He'd never disrespect his older brother like that—which was wildly disappointing for me. I wasn't a cheater, and I never would be, but if Cain asked me to leave Brent for him, I wouldn't think twice.

Hell, if Cain asked me to leave Brent in general, I probably would.

I cared about Brent, I truly did. I loved him. I just wasn't sure if I was *in love* with him. How could I be when my heart beats for another man? His *brother*.

"You think crawling into my brother's bed is a threat? Cain is loyal to me, Rosie. He'd kick you out on your ass faster than you could blink," Brent spat, dropping onto his bed and crossing his legs at his ankles. He locked his hands beneath his head, his elbows sprawled, looking as relaxed as could be.

"I'm not sure why I bother with you, Brent. But I'm over this bullshit. You asked me to move to this freaking city with you, knowing I wouldn't have a job or a place to live. I'm done. Find yourself some other girl to fuck with." Lucky for me, my suitcase had never been unpacked because the jackass didn't have extra space for my shit in his dresser. All I had to grab was my phone charger and bathroom stuff.

Walking across the hall, I grabbed my makeup and hair care products, cradling them in my arms as I made sure I didn't leave anything behind.

I wasn't positive where I'd go tonight, but I'd figure it out. I always did.

Tossing everything into my suitcase, I zipped it up and expanded the handle to roll it out. "Last chance to be a gentleman, Brent."

"Nah," he said without looking at me, pulling out his phone.

My eyes narrowed into slits and my head bobbed as I watched him scroll mindlessly as though I wasn't even in the room anymore. Tilting the suitcase, I rolled it behind me as I walked out of his bedroom.

The hallway was dark, the house quiet, as I moved through the small space toward the front door. When I reached for the knob, a deep voice sounded from the shadowed living room beside me.

"Rosie," Cain called. He sat on the couch in the dark, his face illuminated by the soft moonlight flowing in through the window.

"What, Cain?" What was there to even say? His brother was in the next room, probably listening for the sound of the door closing. This wasn't the first time we'd broken up, or the first time Cain had wanted to say something as I walked out the door after a fight with his brother. But like every other time, Cain said nothing and stared at me from his spot on the couch, his eyes blazing with unspoken words. The rigidness of his features told me he had heard mine and Brent's exchange and he hadn't liked what he heard.

Turning my head back to the door, I twisted the knob and walked out.

When it closed behind me, I didn't bother looking back. Instead, I held my head high and walked down the path, using my key fob to pop open the trunk of my car. The sound of small rocks crunching beneath the wheels of my suitcase battled against my heartbeat that echoed in my ears.

I was so frustrated with Brent and how I let him toss me to the side *again*, and how Cain let his brother treat me like shit and didn't speak up, *again*. I guess it wasn't fair of me to act like Cain really had any authority to say anything, but what woman didn't want a knight in shining armor on occasion? I guess I wouldn't be getting that from either of the Michaels brothers.

"Rosie!"

*Maybe I spoke too soon.*

Cain's voice cut through my inner battle with myself as I tossed my suitcase into the trunk of my blacked-out Honda Accord.

"What do you want, Cain?"

"Come back inside. Please."

"For what? So Brent can give me more details about how he's going to screw someone else and have me listen? Or so you can sit silently while he talks shit? As much as I love being the source of your entertainment, I think I'll pass." I slammed the trunk harder than necessary and rounded the car, pulling open the driver's side door—but I didn't get in. Like a true glutton for punishment, I watched him from over the roof of the car, waiting for him to say something.

Cain rubbed his tattooed hand across the back of his neck, looking down at the ground. After several tense seconds, he brought his attention back to me. "Where are you going?" he asked, taking a few more steps toward my car.

"I don't know," I admitted, my eyes narrowing as I tried thinking about where my first stop would be. Probably the motel on the outskirts of Ridgewood. It'd be the most inexpensive. My heart hammered in my chest as I made a snap decision to pull down one more layer of vulnerability I couldn't really afford to gamble with. "Come with me."

Cain's eyes darkened with my request, and instantly I could see the turmoil behind his light brown eyes. "It's not that easy. Brent's my brother..."

"He'll get over it," I argued, doing my best to keep the desperation out of my voice. I knew I was walking a fine line between being vulnerable and being desperate. I *wasn't* desperate, but Cain held a piece of my heart in his hand and I'd be lying if I denied that I wanted him to run away with me.

"We both know he wouldn't, he'd—"

"Cain? The fuck are you doing?" The screen flew open and hit against the side of the house as Brent's voice boomed from across the front yard. Cain's spine went ramrod straight.

Brent's eyes bounced between me and his brother, narrowing as he assessed us, drawing his own conclusions. Being unapologetically myself, I tossed him a snarky smile, knowing he was about to either explode on both of us, or turn around and slam the door in our faces.

Cain turned to face his brother, shrugging nonchalantly. "She ran from the house like a bat outta hell. I came to find out why."

"Not so sure it looks that way from where I'm standing, *brother*."

Resting my hands on my hips, I watched the two men face off, one looking skeptical while the other looked like he was trying to come up with an iron-clad excuse to save his own ass.

"Not sure what you think it looks like, but I was just making sure your bitch knew to respect our property next time she walked out of the house. She slammed the door so hard it rattled the front windows," Cain spouted, the lies tumbling from his mouth effortlessly as he turned back to me and his features hardened.

"She isn't my bitch anymore," Brent scoffed, stomping down the two steps of the weathered front porch. "Kind of seems like you want her to be your bitch, though."

A satisfied smile curled at my lips—my earlier suggestion of crawling into Cain's bed had clearly resonated with Brent. It got him thinking. Doubting himself and his brother's loyalty.

My intention was never to cause a rift between them, but rather remind Brent that being in his presence was *my* choice. Despite my current lack of income, I knew my damn worth, and with the snap of my fingers, I could have another man lined up if I wanted.

My smile was short-lived though, because nothing could have prepared me for Cain's response, and the wound it would ultimately leave on my heart.

Cain tossed his head back and laughed. What was normally a rare, yet beautiful sound with the power to inflate my heart, came out villainous and cruel. "Why the fuck would I want your sloppy seconds, Brent?" His eyes connected with mine as he delivered the final blow that would ricochet through my darkest moments for years to come. "She's nothing but damaged goods. Trailer trash. You couldn't pay me to give her my cock."

I knew words could hurt, but I hadn't realized just how badly until then.

Without hesitating, I flung myself into the driver's seat and cranked the ignition, not bothering to let it warm up before I tossed the car into drive and sped away, my tires squealing against the asphalt. I blew through the stop sign at the corner of their street, needing to get as far away from the Michaels brothers as quickly as I could. It took everything I had not to glance in the rearview mirror as I hightailed it out of their neighborhood and in the direction of the most expensive hotel in Ridgewood.

Forget staying at a cheap motel. I had some money tucked away, stashed because my subconscious *knew* something like this could happen, and I couldn't think of a more perfect reason to pull a little cash out.

A high thread count and some room service would be exactly what I needed while I licked my wounds for the night.

Why would I sit around in a crappy room and dwell on the words of two certified jerks? Tomorrow was a new day with back-to-back job interviews and a whole lot of promise for my future.

Glass half full, right?

Fuck Brent, and fuck his brother even more.

I was Rosie Adler, and if there was one thing I'd learned over the years, it was that the only person on this planet I needed was myself.

Certainly not a six foot four, tattooed, sexy as sin man who looked like he could murder your enemies with his bare hands, but around you was a complete marshmallow.

Definitely *not* Cain Michaels.

# CHAPTER TWO

*Rosie*

*Present Day*

"*Fuck*, mia preferita, you feel amazing," Sly grunted as he slammed into me, his beautiful Italian accent even thicker during sex. He reached his large hand up and kneaded my boob. "God, I'm so close. I don't think I can hold it much longer. You...feel like paradiso."

My legs wrapped tighter around his body and joined at the ankles as I attempted to shift the pressure to stimulate my clit. Not that I hadn't already orgasmed. But twice never hurt.

Sly's grunts and groans filled the air as he drilled into me, a thin layer of sweat coating his back like he'd been running a marathon. We'd only been at it for less than five minutes, but his chest heaved with exertion.

I did my part in letting out small moans at the right times, digging my nails into his back. I was good at

pretending to be super into it—I'd had enough practice at
faking it over the years. Thankfully, Sly couldn't see me
rolling my eyes and glancing at the diamond Rolex I hadn't
bothered taking off when we got naked.

It wasn't his fault I was bored. My head wasn't in it—I
was tired and stressed, more in the mood to be alone than
to be naked and sweaty, but I'd hoped a good romp in the
sheets would take my mind off the world around me.

Two more grunts and a slam later, Sly's rutting was over.
His body fell to a heap on top of mine and I allowed him
around sixty seconds of caressing before I gave him the
boot. "Alright, Sly, off."

His gaze slid to mine as I stared up at him. He smirked,
dipping down to kiss the side of my mouth, his dick
twitching inside of me before he slid out. He rolled off my
body and dropped onto the bed.

"Sorprendente," he muttered, his voice soft. Bastard
had already tossed an arm over his eyes as if he was going
to fall asleep immediately.

I reached over to pull a cigarette off the nightstand and
lit it up. The cherry glowed red as it caught, and I tossed
the lighter aside. Filling my lungs, I let my eyes close as I
willed myself to relax.

Anxiety crept into my chest, sitting heavily. No sooner
had I inhaled a second puff, Sly pulled it from between my
lips and stuck it between his.

This was our ritual. We fucked, played pass the cig, and
we passed out.

Well, correction, he passed out. Some nights I laid

there for hours until I fell asleep. Other nights, I left and went home.

It wasn't that I didn't enjoy being with Sly, because I truly did. He was great. There was nothing I could pinpoint that made me dislike him, which was why I couldn't figure out why my feelings for him weren't stronger.

Being with him was easy and secure. At all times, I knew where I stood with him and after so many failed relationships, a man like Sly was exactly what I needed. A great lover with a wicked tongue, easy on the eyes, and extremely compliant. Whatever I wanted, I got—the man had never so much as thought the word no when it came to me.

It didn't hurt that he also looked hot as hell in his black jeans and leather vest. Just seeing him on his motorcycle, his bronzed skin covered in tattoos, his dark hair always combed to perfection, and the way he could wear a pair of dark aviators, was enough to get me wet.

I never would have guessed I'd be into the whole motorcycle club thing, but here we were. The best part— Sly never tried to lock me down. He took me at face value and never forced me to commit to a label I wasn't interested in. I wasn't his girlfriend; he wasn't my boyfriend. The simplicity of our arrangement was what kept me from going stir-crazy.

Finishing the cigarette, I watched Sly peel the condom from his limp dick, knot it, and toss it onto the nightstand next to its wrapper. My face contorted as I outwardly cringed, grossed out that he just tossed it haphazardly onto the same surface he puts things like his phone on.

And *he* made fun of *me* for taking a disinfectant wipe to everything the second I stepped foot into his room. I wasn't a germaphobe, but bikers—*men*—could be absolutely fucking disgusting.

I kept my mouth shut and made a mental note to wipe it down at some point while settling into the softness of the cotton sheets. As my eyes shut, I felt his hand circle my middle, and he pulled me closer. There would be no falling asleep for me. His body heat was stifling.

His arm draped across my naked tits, while he gripped my waist and tucked me into his body. *Little spoon.* All I could think about was rolling out from under his grasp.

I *hated* cuddling.

After what felt like hours, the steady rhythm of his breathing told me he was finally asleep. Peeling his fingers from my areola, I scooted my body away and silently placed my feet on the cool hardwood below. I sat for a minute, listening to the low snores as they fell from his lips.

I really did like the man, but there was just something lacking that I couldn't put my finger on. Sly was all golden retriever vibes. And there was nothing wrong with that. Wasn't that what most women wanted? A loyal, loving man who spoiled them? I should want that too.

Maybe the problem was me.

Retrieving my thong, bra, and the men's button down I had worn as a dress today, I quickly got dressed, leaving the shirt unbuttoned. Grabbing another cigarette and my purse, I headed for the door. As I slipped through the crack just wide enough for my body, I lit up another smoke. The cherry was the only illumination in the dark hallway, and as the door clicked closed behind me, I leaned against it with my eyes shut, enjoying a drag.

"That shit will kill you, Rose."

His voice made me jump, not realizing someone else was in the hallway with me. I turned my head to the right where his voice had come from, and watched him push off the wall and stalk toward my direction.

Stopping in front of me, he plucked the cigarette from between my fingers and carelessly tossed it to the floor, snuffing it out with the sole of his boot. "You need to fuckin' quit."

"And you need to quit stalking me, Cain," I retorted, crossing my arms in front of my chest. His eyes trailed down my body, appreciating the swell of my tits, the curves of my wide hips, and the lack of thigh gap. All so different from the body of the girl he once knew.

The Rosie I had been...the Rosie I was...she wasn't me. She was the shiny exterior I showed the world, but I was tired of being her.

While some old habits die hard (and are super challenging to let go of), I was able to control my body.

Life had been crazy over the last two years and I'd decided I needed a change.

Oh, who was I kidding? My life has always been crazy, and I was constantly making changes to myself. But it was within the last couple of years, while watching two of my best friends find their happiness, I realized *I* wasn't happy.

Growing up, my biggest hardship was low self-esteem and an unhealthy relationship with binge eating. Eventually, I fell into the other extreme and became good friends with a little plague called the starvation diet. I trained my body to survive on water-based foods and extremely lean proteins (every once in a while) while I also obsessively killed myself in the gym.

For years I was a slender little minx, but it cost me my happiness.

I conformed to what I thought I needed to look like for society—what I needed to look like to fit into my "bad girl reputation" I had so eloquently placed upon myself. Slender. Dark hair. Big tits. Tattoos.

For what?

That was the million dollar question, and let me just tell you, it wasn't worth a goddamn penny.

Once I had my come to Jesus moment and realized I didn't need to be anyone other than myself, I said goodbye to the salads I forced down my throat and reacquainted myself with carbs. And if people didn't like it, they could promptly fuck off.

Then, I spent a small fortune at the salon to turn my jet-black hair back to my natural—*or as close as I could get to it*—brunette. I even treated myself to a few extra tattoos, because why the hell not?

Instead of a size four, I was now more of a comfortable eight/ten, and I loved myself more than ever.

So when Cain's gaze finally reconnected with mine, I jutted my chin out with confidence and gave him my award-winning attitude. "Why the hell are you out here? Enjoying the audio-version of the porn you'll never get to watch?"

His smirk made my stomach turn. The jury was still out on whether it was a good "butterflies" type or bad "want to upchuck all over him" type of turn.

Probably a little of both.

Cain, unfortunately, caused the butterflies in my stomach to flutter whenever I caught sight of him, which seemed to be more frequent lately. He'd aged like a fine wine. Thirty-five years old and a fine specimen of a man. He was covered head to toe in black and gray tattoos—at least I was sure he was. I hadn't ever seen him completely naked, but had seen him without his shirt many, many times. He had that rugged appearance that made my toes curl. His coffee brown hair was always messily pulled back into a bun at the crown of his head, and his facial hair was always scruffy, but in a way that worked for him. He had the zero effort thing down and in his favor. Add that to his blue jeans, t-shirt, and leather vest decked out with club insignia—*damn*, he was fine.

An ass, but pretty to look at.

"Hearing you *fake it* was the highlight of my night, Rose," he told me, his voice thick with sarcasm.

I flipped him the bird before pushing off the door I still leaned against. Giving him my back, I walked down the pitch-black hallway. Not many people were up in the bedrooms yet, it was hardly midnight, but Sly and I had snuck off earlier in the night. The vibration from the bass of the speakers rattled the walls from the music playing in the bar on the floor below us. "Stop calling me Rose," I called over my shoulder.

Cain's footsteps were heavy behind me as he followed. "Where are you hurrying off to?"

I took the opportunity of being cloaked in darkness to button my shirt. My feet were bare and I moved quietly, but he was hardly three steps behind me. When I made it to the back staircase, I stopped and turned to him, turning on the fake charm. "What do you want, Cainy-boo?"

I ran my finger down the soft leather of his vest and along the waistband of his jeans. My sarcasm didn't go unnoticed, and he boxed me in, caging me as my back pressed against the cool wooden banister.

"You know, *Rose*, your attitude isn't as off-putting as you think." He traced his nose against my cheek, tipping his lips toward my ear. "I *see* you," he whispered softly.

My body betrayed me, and a shiver ran over my skin. The cocky bastard knew it too, because he added, "I know this isn't one-sided. You're just fucking around with Sly and buying time until I finally claim you."

"You can't claim a woman who wants nothing to do with you, Cain."

"Your body seems to disagree with that statement."

"It's cold in here, asshole. My goosebumps are for lack of warmth, not lack of dick. We both know I'm not lacking in the latter, so just go ahead and fuck off back to where you came from."

He tipped his head back and released a husky laugh. "Hell hath no fury like a woman scorned, right, Rose?"

"To have fury toward you, Cain, would imply I care. Which I don't. Truly."

"Your words pain me, baby."

"Actions speak louder than words, Cain. Although you seem to have a knack for making your words pretty damn loud."

His features turned dark and his mood sobered. No longer smirking and laughing, I could see the fire behind Cain's eyes as he searched my face, looking for a glimmer of sarcasm or playfulness to indicate I wasn't being serious. But I was.

I forced myself to hold my own, to mask the feeling of inadequacy threatening to show on my face. As memories pushed their way to the forefront of my mind, I could feel the hurt surfacing.

*No.*

I looked away, but something must have trickled across my face, causing Cain to take a step back. "Rose, you know I didn't mean what I fucking said. I had to say it to save face in front of Brent."

Whipping my head back toward him, I snarled, "You knew how I felt about you, Cain. And you knew how he treated me. Yet you still sat there and called me—*to my face*—what was it again? Damaged goods, trailer trash? Wait... No... That wasn't all you said."

"You know I had to. If he knew I was after his girl, he would have murdered me. He would have murdered *us*."

"Bullshit, Cain. Brent and I were so on-again off-again, he wouldn't have cared either way. When I walked away from him for good last year, he didn't come running. Plus, *we* never did anything. You and I were nothing but unexplored feelings and lustful looks across the room. It's never been about your actions. In this case, Cain, it was about *your* words. How *you* treated me. I expected better from you. You were always the nice one."

"He's my fucking brother, Rose. What was I supposed to do?"

"It doesn't matter what you should have done, because you did nothing. And now, I want *nothing* to do with you. I've let it go, Cain. Moved on. You should too."

Without waiting for his reply, I ducked beneath the arm keeping me caged against the banister, and took the stairs down two at a time, not sparing him a backward glance as I pushed open the door to the main floor of *my* bar, Andromeda.

Printed in the USA
CPSIA information can be obtained
at www.ICGtesting.com
JSHW021049230324
59770JS00005B/37

9 798869 188625